Amy Goff
Illustrated by Lucy Tanner-Duckham

To My Lockdown Baby

BUMBLEBEE PAPERBACK EDITION
Copyright © Amy Goff 2023
Illustrations by Lucy Tanner-Duckham

The right of Amy Goff to be identified as author of
this work has been asserted in accordance with sections 77 and 78 of the Copyright, Designs and
Patents Act 1988.

All Rights Reserved

No reproduction, copy or transmission of this publication
may be made without written permission.
No paragraph of this publication may be reproduced,
copied or transmitted save with the written permission of the publisher, or in accordance with the
provisions
of the Copyright Act 1956 (as amended).

Any person who commits any unauthorised act in relation to
this publication may be liable to criminal
prosecution and civil claims for damage.

A CIP catalogue record for this title is
available from the British Library.

ISBN: 978-1-83934-650-7
Bumblebee Books is an imprint of
Olympia Publishers.

First Published in 2023

Bumblebee Books
Tallis House
2 Tallis Street
London
EC4Y 0AB

Printed in Great Britain

Dedication

I dedicate this book to my beautiful boy, Frankie.

I'd planned to show you the world.

So you could see,

smell

and explore everything around you.

We'd have visits from family and friends. Endless cuddles for both of us.

I'd planned our first adventure...

and trips to the seaside.

I'd planned playdates with your friends...

But the world closed its doors.
It was just you and me.

The days were long, and the nights were longer.

We laughed,

we cried, life didn't go as planned.

But we had each other and so we made it through.

You gave me every cuddle I could have needed and I gave you yours.

You were the light that kept me going. Every dark day I was thankful I had you.

Whenever I felt sad, I'd look at you and you'd remind me I had all I needed.

You gave me a reason to smile every day,

every giggle and every hug was mine.

Lockdown baby, it wasn't easy, but I'd do it all again... just to have you.

About the Author

Amy is a first-time author who became a single mum to her son during lockdown. Amy has now gone onto to train as a coach; using her experiences to empower single mums to heal from their past, learn to love themselves again and live the life they deserve. You can find out more through Amy's instagram: @amy.goff

Acknowledgements

Thank you to my mum and sister, without their love and support throughout, this wouldn't have been possible.